THE
BARNABUS
PROJECT

By Terry, Eric & Devin Fan

tundra

Barnabus lived in a secret lab.
He was half mouse and half elephant,
and he had lived in the lab as long as he could remember.

The lab was hidden beneath Perfect Pets
on a perfectly ordinary street.

It was deep underground,
where no one would
ever find it.

The lab was where they made Perfect Pets.

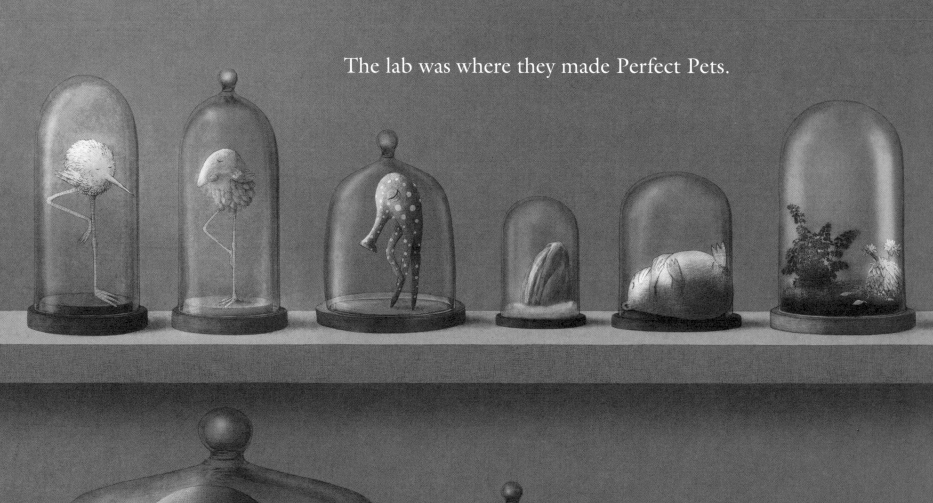

Except Barnabus wasn't quite perfect.

He had been put in a part of the lab called Failed Projects.

His home was rather small, but that just meant it was easier to keep tidy.

The Green Rubber Suits always fed Barnabus his favorite food, which was cheese and peanuts.

And yet,
he sometimes
wondered about
the world outside
of his little bell jar.

It was Pip the cockroach who told them stories about the world above.

Stories about a sparkling silver lake,
green trees, and mountains that reached
all the way to the sky, lit with their own stars.

"Maybe someday I'll sit on the grass
and look at the stars," said Barnabus.

And when he closed his eyes, he almost could.

"Impossible," said Pip.

"Nothing is impossible," said Barnabus.
But secretly he worried his friend might be right.

At that moment, the Green Rubber Suits came in.

They turned on the lights and
checked each bell jar one by one.

They made strange noises
to each other.

They peered
and they poked.

They peeked
and they prodded.

They put red stamps on all the jars.

Then they left.

"What does it mean?"
said Barnabus, looking up
at the strange red stamp.

"It means you're going
to be recycled," said Pip.
"That's what happens
to all Failed Projects."

"You'll be fluffier afterwards,"
offered Pip kindly.

"And you'll be cuter,
and your eyes will
probably be bigger."

"I like having small eyes," said Barnabus,
although he wasn't even sure anymore.

Barnabus slumped in his jar.

He wasn't fluffy enough, and his eyes were beady,
but he liked himself just the way he was.

And what if, after he was recycled, peanuts
and cheese were no longer his favorite foods?

What if his friends didn't recognize him after?

What if he no longer cared about green trees
and mountains lit with their own stars?

"We need to escape!" said Barnabus suddenly.
The other Failed Projects gasped, but then they cheered.
"Impossible," said Pip.

"Nothing is impossible," said Barnabus.

He took a step back . . .

. . . and he kicked as hard as he could.

He charged at the glass.

But the bell jar was much
stronger than he was.

Finally, Barnabus made a
sad sound with his trunk.

A tiny crack appeared!

He was free!

Then he freed the others: the Dust Bunnies, Lite-Up Lois, Bumble Bear, the Amotax, Mushroom Sloth, Wally the Ripple, Stick One and Stick Two, Quirt, Moshi, Pompidou, Furtle, Blinky, the Bottle Mogs, Lowell, Percival, Spike, Pinto, Chloe, Peep, Leaf. All of them.

You have to understand, they had never been outside of their
jars before. There was quite a commotion. They whooped and sang.
They chirped and hooted. They stretched their legs and jumped for joy.

When they calmed down a bit,
they peeked over the edge.
The floor was far below.

"Now what?" said Quirt.

"We have to work together,"
said Barnabus.

One by one they
helped each other down . . .

. . . until they finally reached the floor.
"Shhhhh!" said Barnabus, and they all fell silent.

Then they heard it too.

Footsteps in the corridor outside.

"Quick!" said Barnabus. "We can go through here."

He didn't like dark places, but the footsteps were getting closer.

Everyone crawled into the vent
with Lite-Up Lois leading the way.

It was a tight squeeze for some of them.

The vent led into the most secret part of the secret lab.

They all looked up.

"We need to RUN!" cried Pip.

But Barnabus couldn't run.
The great, sad eye seemed to
be looking directly at him.

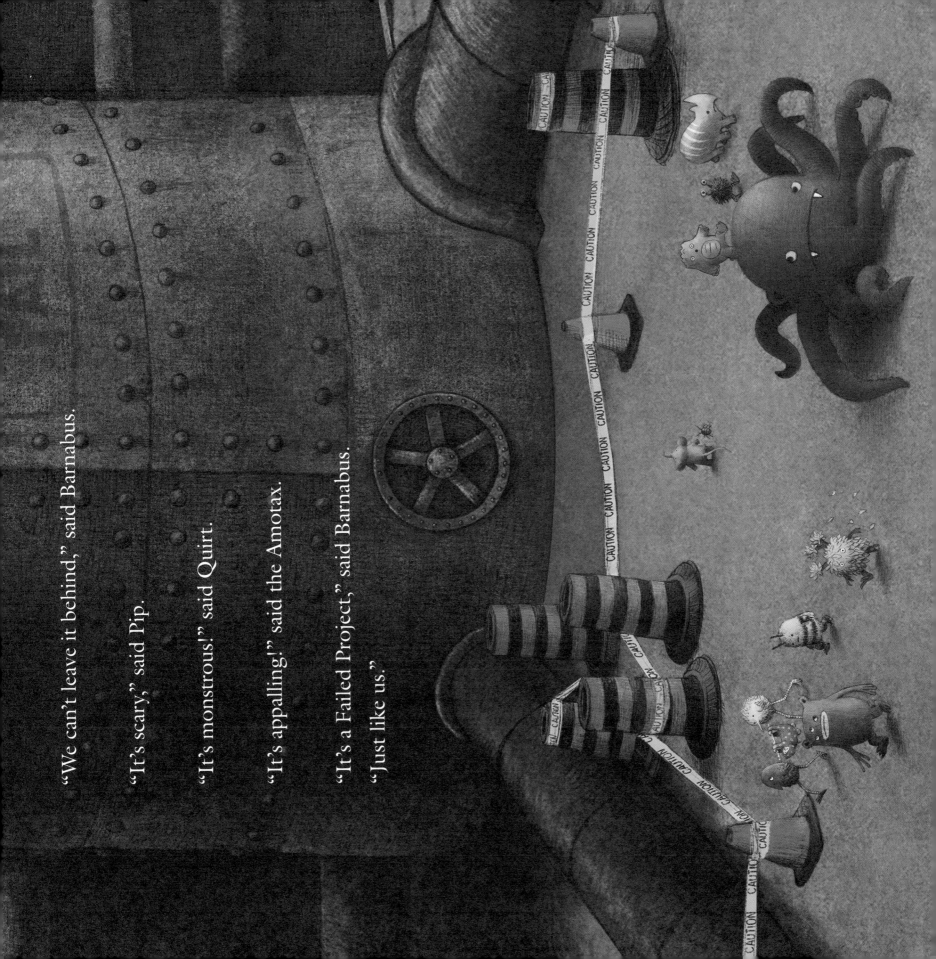

"We can't leave it behind," said Barnabus.

"It's scary," said Pip.

"It's monstrous!" said Quirt.

"It's appalling!" said the Amotax.

"It's a Failed Project," said Barnabus.

"Just like us."

They worked together to turn the great valve that opened the tank.

But it was too late . . .

The Green Rubber Suits had found them!

Just when all seemed lost, the tank doors swung open and water flooded into the lab.

Up the water carried them . . .

Up to the world above.

When they finally opened their eyes, they were
in a puddle, surrounded by shelves of Perfect Pets.

Everyone ran towards the exit . . .

Barnabus stopped.

It was almost like looking in a mirror,
except Barnaby's eyes were bigger, and his fur
was like cotton candy.

He was perfect.

"Barnabus!" Pip called from the front of the store.
"Look! It's the outside world!"

Barnabus ran to join his friends.
He might not be perfect . . .

But he was free!

The world was much bigger than Barnabus and his friends
ever could have imagined.

And just like Pip said, there were mountains that
reached to the sky, lit with their own stars.

"You were right," said Pip.
"Nothing is impossible."

Soon they found a place full of sunshine
and happy noises, green trees and soft grass.

A place that might be home.

It wasn't always easy . . .

But they always stuck together.

LITTLE CHEEP

10 UNIQUE MELODIES!

PERFECT PETS

BIG CHEEP

20 UNIQUE MELODIES!!

PERFECT PETS

POM POM

BLOWS BUBBLES!

PERFECT PETS

CHIP

PERFECT PETS

MOOP

PERFECT PETS

PSSSST... IT SPEAKS IN WHISTLES!

SPROUT

PERFECT PETS

JUST ADD WATER!

WANDA THE RIPPLE!

PERFECT PETS

BUMBLE

★ STAR ★

PERFECT PETS

GLITTER POPS

PERFECT PETS

SUPER SLIME

GLOW-IN-THE-DARK!

NOW EVEN SLIMIER!

PERFECT PETS

SQUIRT

SUBMERSIBLE!

PERFECT PETS